Winning
with Teamwork

Compiled by
Katherine Karvelas
Successories, Inc., Editorial Coordinator

CAREER PRESS
3 Tice Road, P. O. Box 687
Franklin Lakes, NJ 07417
1-800-CAREER-1; 201-848-0310 (NJ and outside U. S.)
FAX: 201-848-1727

WINNING WITH TEAMWORK
Cover design by Successories
Typesetting by Eileen Munson
Printed in the U.S.A. by Book-mart Press

To order this title, please call toll-free 1-800-CAREER-1 (NJ and
Canada: 201-848-0310) to order using VISA or MasterCard, or for
further information on books from Career Press.

Library of Congress Cataloging-in-Publication Data

Winning with teamwork : quotations to inspire the power of teamwork /
    by editors of Successories.
        p.   cm.
    ISBN 1-56414-388-0 (pbk.)
    1. Teams in the workplace--Quotations, maxims, etc. 2. Teamwork
(Sports)--Quotations, maxims, etc.   I. Successories.
HD66.W563   1998
658.4' 036--dc21
                                                    98-28302

Introduction

The search for personal and professional success is a lifelong journey of trial and error. This inspiring collection of wit and wisdom is a celebration of life's lessons. Each saying is a motivational push to stay on track of your goals and pursue your dreams.

In these pages you will find more than 300 powerful and compelling quotations from a diverse group of people—business professionals, writers, activists, actors, artists, sports professionals, scientists, philosophers, politicians, and everyday people who inspire us.

This unique collection was compiled after years of insightful reading and warm discussions with people who were kind enough to share their personal collections of quotations. Working on this book has been an enlightening and gratifying experience. We hope reading these quotes will be an equally gratifying and motivating experience for you on your journey of success.

In a team sport like basketball,
every time you help somebody
else, you help yourself.

Pete Carrill

Working together works.

Dr. Rob Gilbert

The secret is to work less as
individuals and more as a team. As
a coach, I play not my eleven best,
but my best eleven.

Knute Rockne

Either we're pulling together or
we're pulling apart.

Anonymous

Setting a goal is not the main
thing. It is deciding how you will
go about achieving it and staying
with that plan.

Tom Landry

The country is full of good
coaches. What it takes to win is
a bunch of interested players.

Don Coryell

Together we can change the world.

Anonymous

You can't do it alone. Be a team player, not an individualist, and respect your teammates. Anything you do, you'll have to do as a team. Many records have been made, but only because of the help of one's teammates.

Charley Taylor

Little disciplines multiply rewards.

Jim Rohn

T*eamwork is absolutely essential to winning football games. Football is not a one-man game, but a team undertaking, a team endeavor. Each man must be willing to sacrifice personal ambition for the good of the team.*

Bert Jones

Sticks in a bundle are unbreakable.

Kenyan proverb

There are precious few Einsteins among us. Most brilliance arises from ordinary people working together in extraordinary ways.

Roger von Oech

Skill and confidence are an unconquered army.

George Herbert

Continuity of purpose is one of
the most essential ingredients of
happiness in the long run, and
for most men this comes chiefly
through their work.

Bertrand Russell

When men are rightly occupied,
their amusement grows out of their
work, as the color-petals out of a
fruitful flower.

John Ruskin

You become successful by helping
others become successful.

Anonymous

Once you learn how good you
really are, you never settle for
playing less than your best.

Reggie Jackson

All happiness depends on courage
and work.

Honoré de Balzac

Large-scale success today is spelled "Teamwork." The successful teamworker doesn't wear a chip on his shoulder, doesn't look for slights, isn't constantly on the alert lest his "dignity" be insulted. He puts the good of the house—the company or team—first. And if the whole prospers, he, as an active, effective, progressive part, will prosper with it.

B. C. Forbes

One man's word is no man's word;
we should quietly hear all sides.

Anonymous

Never doubt that a small group of
thoughtful citizens can change the
world. Indeed, it is the only thing
that ever has.

Margaret Mead

To accept good advice from others
increases one's own ability.

Anonymous

Anything one man can imagine,
other men can make real.

Jules Verne

One man can't do it alone. Football
is a team sport. A running back is
only as good as his offensive line.

Greg Pruitt

Doing nothing for others is the
undoing of ourselves.

Horace Mann

A company is known by the people it keeps.

Anonymous

Every great person is always being helped by everybody; for his gift is to get good out of all things and all persons.

John Ruskin

Praise loudly and blame softly.

Catherine II

Now this is the law of the jungle—

As old and as true as the sky;

And the wolf that keep it may prosper,

But the wolf that shall break it must die.

As the creeper that girdles the tree trunk,

The law runneth forward and back—

And the strength of the pack is the wolf

And the strength of the wolf is the pack.

Rudyard Kipling

As a rule of thumb, involve
everyone in everything.

Tom Peters

In the heroic organizations, people
mentor each other unselfishly.

Anonymous

Winners can tell you where they
are going, what they are doing,
what they plan to do along the way,
and who will be sharing the
adventure with them.

Denis Waitley

Give all the credit away.

John Wooden

I am proud of all my trophies, but
truthfully when I was playing, I
never thought of records. I just
tried to do all I possibly could to
help the team win.

Roy Campanella

We are in this life together.

Anonymous

No matter what accomplishments
you make, somebody helps you.

Wilma Rudolph

If you're too busy to help those
around you succeed, you're too
busy.

Anonymous

It is only as we develop others that
we permanently succeed.

Harvey Firestone

The heights by great men

reached and kept

Were not attained by sudden flight,

But they, while their

companions slept,

Were toiling upward in the night.

Henry Wadsworth Longfellow

The best thing to hold onto in life
is each other.

Anonymous

I think we may safely trust a good
deal more than we do.

Henry David Thoreau

Asking for help is a strength, not a
weakness.

Anonymous

Build for your team a feeling of
oneness, of dependence on one
another, and of strength to be
derived by unity.

Vince Lombardi

Joys divided are increased.

Josia Gilbert Holland

Nothing great will ever be achieved
without great men, and men are
great only if they are determined
to be so.

Charles de Gaulle

There is no letter "I" in the word teamwork.

Bill Foster

Quarterbacks don't win or lose football games. Teams do.

Fran Tarkenton

I've learned one important thing about living. I can do anything I think I can—but I can't do anything alone.

Dr. Robert Schuller

Try to forget yourself in the service of others. For when we think too much of ourselves and our own interests, we easily become despondent. But when we work for others, our efforts return to bless us.

Sidney Powell

If everyone is moving forward together, then the success takes care of itself.

Henry Ford

None of us is as smart as all of us.

Ken Blanchard

The best team doesn't win nearly as often as the team that gets along best.

Dr. Rob Gilbert

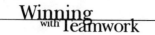

The team player knows that it doesn't matter who gets the credit as long as the job gets done. If the job gets done, the credit will come.

Anonymous

Those conquer who endure.

Persius

A few mistakes don't worry me; what worries me is when you make the mistakes and then forget your role on the team and start to worry about your ego.

Digger Phelps

There is no exercise better for the heart than reaching down and lifting people up.

John A. Holmes

To promote cooperation remember: People tend to resist that which is forced upon them. People tend to support that which they help to create.

Vince Pfaff

Winners never quit and quitters never win.

Anonymous

Working together, ordinary people can perform extraordinary feats. They can push things that come into their hands a little higher up, a little further on towards the heights of excellence.

Anonymous

People who are unable to motivate themselves must be content with mediocrity, no matter how impressive their other talents.

Andrew Carnegie

Team spirit is a competitive advantage.

Anonymous

Work as hard as you possibly can within the team structure.

Red Holzman

Teamwork divides the task and doubles the success.

Anonymous

He who trusts men will make fewer mistakes than he who distrusts them.

Camille di Cavour

Deal with the faults of others as gently as with your own.

Chinese proverb

Our future will be a reflection of
our teamwork.

Anonymous

The achievements of an
organization are the result of the
combined effort of each individual.

Vince Lombardi

No one can whistle a symphony. It
takes an orchestra to play it.

H. E. Luccock

World's greatest management
principle: You can work miracles
by having faith in others. To
get the best out of people,
choose to think and believe
the best about them.

Anonymous

A successful team comes from
mutual recognition.

Anonymous

I'm only a reflection of what our
team is.

Jim Zorn

Trust men and they will be true to
you, treat them greatly and they
will show themselves great.

Ralph Waldo Emerson

Many people with one voice will
always speak louder than many
people with many voices.

Anonymous

Appreciation is a wonderful thing; it
makes what is excellent in others
belong to us as well.

Voltaire

Never look down on anybody unless
you're helping him up.

Jesse Jackson

Trust is the emotional glue that binds a team together.

Anonymous

Only a life lived for others is worth living.

Albert Einstein

Working together is essential for success; even freckles would make a nice tan if they would get together.

Anonymous

On the set, I like everyone to eat together, share food and stories, and kid and joke because some of that comes over into the working day. The comfort you establish among each other shows on the screen.

Alan Alda

Ask not what your teammates can do for you. Ask what you can do for your teammates.

Magic Johnson

Those who act receive the prizes.

Aristotle

The greatest thing in this world is not so much where we are, but in what direction we are moving.

Oliver Wendell Holmes

Relationships of trust depend
on our willingness to look not
only to our own interests, but
also the interests of others.

Peter Farquharson

One guy can't win the Stanley
Cup or the Boston Bruins
would have won it seven
straight years with Bobby Orr.
The better the team plays, the
better you play.

Wayne Gretzky

A noble person attracts noble people, and knows how to hold on to them.

Goethe

Ingenuity, plus courage, plus work, equals miracles.

Bob Richards

When love and skill work together, expect a masterpiece.

John Ruskin

The finest compliment that anyone can pay a person is to say he is a complete team player. To deserve this tribute, your every thought, action, and deed should be one that you are doing for the team.

Jack Pardee

Humankind has not woven the
web of life. We are but one thread
within it. Whatever we do to the
web, we do to ourselves. All things
are bound together. All things
connect.

Chief Seattle

Good work and good companions
are the buildings of great
enterprises.

Anonymous

Successful people breed success.

Anonymous

Those who bring sunshine to the lives of others cannot keep it from themselves.

James M. Barrie

I never perceived myself to be the big star. I'm only one of the nine guys. I think it is good to think that way.

Cal Ripken, Jr.

Nothing is so contagious as
enthusiasm.

Edward George Bulwer-Lytton

Encourage one another. Many
times a word of praise or thanks or
appreciation or cheer has kept
people on their feet.

Charles Swindoll

All men are caught in an
inescapable network of mutuality.

Martin Luther King, Jr.

*An empowered organization
is one in which individuals
have the knowledge, skill,
desire, and opportunity to
personally succeed in a way
that leads to collective
organizational success.*

Stephen R. Covey

Good plans shape good decisions.
That's why good planning helps to
make elusive dreams come true.

Lester R. Bittell

Vital to every worthwhile operation
is cooperation.

Frank Tyger

It is not a question of how well
each person on a team works, the
question is how well they work
together.

Anonymous

Use missteps as stepping stones to
deeper understanding and greater
achievement.

Susan Taylor

To succeed—do the best you can,
where you are, with what you have.

Anonymous

To accomplish great things, we
must not only act, but also dream;
not only plan, but also believe.

Anatole France

No man is an island, entire of itself; every man is a piece of the continent, a part of the main.

John Donne

The race is not always to the swiftest team...but to those who keep on running.

Anonymous

All human power is a compound of time and patience.

Honoré de Balzac

Teamwork is the ability to
work together toward a common
vision. The ability to direct
individual accomplishment
toward organizational objectives.
It is the fuel that allows common
people to attain uncommon
results.

Anonymous

Our objective ought to be to have a
good army rather than a large one.

George Washington

A certain amount of opposition is
good for a team. Kites don't rise
with the wind, but against it.

Doris Pickert

Don't find fault, find a remedy.

Henry Ford

The men who try to do something
and fail are infinitely better than
those who try to do nothing and
succeed.

Lloyd Jones

We must have courage to bet on
our ideas, to take the calculated
risk, and to act.

Maxwell Maltz

The main ingredient of stardom is
the rest of the team.

John Wooden

The man who needs no one's help
is a lonely man indeed.

Dagobert D. Runes

Many of us are more capable than
some of us...but none of us is as
capable as all of us!!

Tom Wilson, "Ziggy"

I always prefer to believe the best
of everybody; it saves so much
trouble.

Rudyard Kipling

Successful teamwork requires doing lots of unspectacular little things, constant attention to the details, building one-on-one relationships, following up on commitments and an obsessive concern for communicating information.

Glenn Parker

The most important trip you may
take in life is meeting people
halfway.

Henry Boye

No man can become rich without
himself enriching others.

Andrew Carnegie

Great accomplishments have
resulted from the transmission of
ideas and enthusiasm.

Thomas J. Watson

We don't work for each other, we work with each other.

Anonymous

No one can be the best at everything. But when all of us combine our talents, we can and will be the best at virtually anything.

Dan Zadra

Teamwork can turn difficulties into opportunities.

Anonymous

Many hands make light work.

English proverb

Three helping one another bear
the burden of six.

George Herbert

The bravest are surely those who
have the clearest vision of what is
before them, glory and danger
alike, and yet notwithstanding, go
out to meet it.

Thucydides

A leader must believe in teamwork through participation. He can never close the gap between himself and the group. He must walk, as it were, a tightrope between the consent he must win and the control he must exert.

Vince Lombardi

Appreciative words are the most
powerful force for good on earth.

George W. Crane

He who wishes to secure the good
of others, has already secured his
own.

Confucius

A combined effort can break down
the wall of impossibility.

Daniel Alexander Triant

Winners are people who do jobs
uncommonly well even when they
don't feel like doing them at all.

Anonymous

If we did all things we are capable
of doing, we would literally
astound ourselves.

Thomas Edison

When great minds get together
and brainstorm, the possibilities
are endless.

Kambo

Successful people use their strength by recognizing, developing, and utilizing the talents of others.

Zig Ziglar

The miracle is this—the more we share, the more we have.

Leonard Nimoy

There is no such thing as a self-made man. You will reach your goals only with the help of others.

George Shinn

One man may hit the mark,
another blunder; but heed not
these distinctions. Only from
the alliance of the one, working
with and through the other, are
great things born.

Antoine de Saint-Exupéry

Some men dream of worthy
accomplishments, while others stay
awake and do them.

Anonymous

We will either find a way, or make
one.

Hannibal

There is no limit to what can be
accomplished when no one cares
who gets the credit.

John Wooden

You get the best out of others when you give the best of yourself.

Harvey Firestone

There is no higher religion than human service. To work for the common good is the greatest creed.

Albert Schweitzer

The character of a team is reflected in the standards they set for themselves.

Anonymous

A committed team can overcome obstacles by pulling together and combining their individual strengths.

Anonymous

Individual commitment to a group effort—that is what makes a team work, a company work, a society work, a civilization work.

Vince Lombardi

Men who have lost heart have never yet won a trophy.

Greek proverb

The point that most needs to be borne in mind is that the welfare of every business is dependent upon cooperation and teamwork on the part of its personnel. Proper cooperation cannot be secured between groups of men who are constantly quarelling among themselves over petty grievances.

Charles Gow

The power of the waterfall is nothing but a lot of drips working together.

Anonymous

We must learn to live together as brothers or perish together as fools.

Martin Luther King, Jr.

No matter how great a warrior he is, a chief cannot do battle without his Indians.

Anonymous

A company with internal
dissension is drained of energy
before it has a chance to devote
itself to its proper purpose.

J. C. Penney

Our greatest glory is not in never
failing, but in rising up every time
we fail.

Ralph Waldo Emerson

Teams with goals succeed because
they know where they're going.

Anonymous

We are what we repeatedly do.
Excellence, therefore, is not an act
but a habit.

Aristotle

No member of a crew is praised for
the rugged individuality of his
rowing.

Ralph Waldo Emerson

Even a goat and an ox must keep
in step if they are going to plough
together.

Ernest Bramah

I *don't get a big charge out of being the leading scorer. The object of competing is winning. I just try to do what has to be done for us to win. That might be anything at any time—defense, rebounding, passing. I get satisfaction out of being a team player.*

Kareem Abdul-Jabbar

A whole bushel of wheat is made
up of single grains.

Thomas Fuller

Never one thing and seldom one
person can make for a success. It
takes a number of them merging
into one perfect whole.

Marie Dressler

The mightiest rivers lost their force
when split up into several streams.

Ovid

Clapping with the right hand only will not produce a noise.

Malay proverb

Trust is the cornerstone in a successful team.

Fran Rees

You can't win if nobody catches the ball in the outfield. You're only as good as the team you have behind you.

Jim Palmer

We treat our people like royalty. If you honor and serve the people who work for you, they will honor and serve you.

Mary Kay Ash

Innovation is simply group intelligence having fun.

Michael Nolan

Diversity: the art of thinking independently together.

Malcolm Forbes

The sports world is a classic example of the game of life. Much can be accomplished when nobody becomes too concerned with who gets the credit. Great plays are made possible by unselfish and disciplined individuals who are more concerned with end results than with personal ones.

Jack Whitaker

It is in supporting one another
that two hands find strength. A
thorny branch can only be cut if
the left hand is helping. The right
hand raised alone could not cut
even a morsel of gristle.

Abdiliaahi Muuse

As an organization grows it must
be more human, not less.

Swift & Co., circa 1920

Positive thinkers grease the axles of
the world.

Anonymous

You don't always have to like each other, but you have to be able to count on each other. When my team calls on me, I'll be ready. When they set the ball down, I'll put it through.

George Blanda

A successful team is the maximum utilization of individual abilities to reach the goal.

Anonymous

Coming together, sharing together, working together, succeeding together.

Anonymous

Many hands make light work.

English proverb

The coach is the team, and the team is the coach. You reflect each other.

Sparky Anderson

The Master Mind Principle: Two or more people actively engaged in pursuit of a definite purpose with a positive mental attitude, constitute an unbeatable force.

Napoleon Hill

No general can fight his battles alone. He must depend upon his lieutenants, and his success depends upon his ability to select the right man for the right place.

L. Ogden Armour

If I have been able to see farther than others, it is because I have stood on the shoulders of giants.

Sir Isaac Newton

There's a misconception about teamwork. Teamwork is the ability to argue and stand up and say loud and strong what you feel. But in the end, it's the ability to adjust to what is best for the team.

Tom Landry

Everyone appreciates being appreciated. Try to catch people red-handed in the act of doing something right—and praise them for it.

Bob Mowad

The object is not to see through
one another, but to see one
another through.

Peter DeVries

Those convinced against their will
are of the same opinion still.

Dale Carnegie

We must always change, renew,
rejuvenate ourselves; otherwise we
harden.

Goethe

We all came together six
months before the 1980 Winter
Olympics with different styles of
hockey and different ethnic
beliefs...but we made ourselves
a team. Individually, we could
not have done it.

Mike Eruzione

Celebrate what you want to see
more of.

Tom Peters

Success is not so much
achievement as achieving.
Refuse to join the cautious crowd
that plays not to lose; play to win.

David J. Mahoney

Working together means winning
together.

Anonymous

In heroic organization, people
mentor each other unselfishly.

Anonymous

There can be hope only for a
society which acts as one big family,
not as many separate ones.

Anwar Sadat

Remember, if you try to go to it
alone, then the fence that shuts
others out shuts you in.

Anonymous

For decades great athletic teams
have harbored one simple secret
that only a few select business
teams have discovered, and it is
this: To play and win together, you
must practice together.

Lewis Edwards

Let us watch well our beginnings,
and results will manage
themselves.

Alexander Clarke

A team of giants needs
giant pitchers who throw good
ideas. But every great pitcher
needs an outstanding catcher.
Without giant catchers, the
ideas of giant pitchers may
eventually disappear.

Max De Pree

T.E.A.M. = Together Everyone
Achieves More.

Anonymous

Your most precious possession is
not your financial assets. Your most
precious possession is the people
you have working there, and what
they carry around in their heads,
and their ability to work together.

Robert Reich

A successful team beats with one heart.

Anonymous

The world basically and fundamentally is constituted on the basis of harmony. Everything works in cooperation with something else.

Preston Bradley

To live is not to live for oneself alone; let us help one another.

Menander of Athens

Be a go-giver as well as a go-getter.

Whitt Schultz

We didn't all come over in the same ship, but we're all in the same boat.

Bernard M. Baruch

Selfishness corrodes. Unselfishness ennobles, satisfies. Don't put off the joy derivable from doing helpful, kindly things for others.

Anonymous

Here is a basic rule for
winning success. Let's mark it
in the mind and remember it.
The rule is: Success depends on
the support of other people. The
only hurdle between you and
what you want to be is the
support of others.

David Joseph Schwartz

Team success and individual
success can be synonymous.

Anonymous

A company is like a ship. Everyone
ought to be prepared to take the
helm.

Morris Weeks

Humor is a great lubricant for
teamwork.

Anonymous

I am only one. I cannot do
everything but I can do something;
and what I can do, that I ought
to do; and what I ought to do, I
shall do.

Edward Everett Hale

A team leader must set an example
for others to follow.

Anonymous

When was ever honey made with
one bee in a hive?

Thomas Hood

Live as brave men; and if fortune is
adverse, front its blows with brave
hearts.

Cicero

If you aren't fired with enthusiasm,
you will be fired with enthusiasm.

Vince Lombardi

Innovation creates opportunity,
quality creates demand, but it takes
teamwork to make it happen.

Anonymous

The only people who achieve much are those who want knowledge so badly that they seek it while the conditions are still unfavorable. Favorable conditions never come.

C. S. Lewis

Hot heads and cold hearts never solved anything.

Billy Graham

Most of us would get along very well if we used the advice we give to others.

Anonymous

When you're through changing, you're through.

Bruce Barton

Make us masters of ourselves that
we may be the servants of others.

Sir Alexander Pope

Example is not the main thing in
influencing others—it is the only
thing.

Albert Schweitzer

To be a successful member of a
team: Do more than you have to
do, more than your share, and do
it as well as you can.

Anonymous

No one does his duty unless he
does his best.

Billy Sunday

People must be able to combine
what they desire with what is
objectively possible and with what
they can subjectively accomplish.

Jurgen Moltmann

Be honorable yourself if you wish
to associate with honorable people.

Welsh proverb

To break through creativity,
we must defer judgment.
That is, learn to accept all
ideas, without prejudice,
and examine them each
in turn.

Scott Isaksen

The work praises the team.

Anonymous

The gates of opportunity and advancement swing on these hinges: initiative, industry, insight, and integrity.

Dr. William Arthur Ward

The best minute you spend is the one you invest in people.

Ken Blanchard

Men of the noblest dispositions think themselves happiest when others share their happiness with them.

Jeremy Taylor

The greater the difficulty the more glory in surmounting it.

Epicurus

All we can ever do in the way of good to people is to encourage them to do good to themselves.

Randolph Bourne

The habits of vigorous minds are formed in contending with difficulties...great necessities call out great virtues.

Abigail Adams

Every kind of peaceful cooperation among men is primarily based on mutual trust.

Albert Einstein

By asking for the impossible we obtain the best possible.

Italian proverb

The way a team plays as a whole determines its success. You may have the greatest bunch of individual stars in the world, but if they don't play together, the club won't be worth a dime.

Babe Ruth

One must be fond of people and
trust them if one is not to make a
mess of life.

E. M. Forster

Never give up on anybody.

Hubert H. Humphrey

Patience, persistence, and
perspiration make an unbeatable
combination of a successful team.

Anonymous

Ideas must work through the brains and the arms of the good and brave, or they are no better than dreams.

Ralph Waldo Emerson

Abilities not used are abilities wasted.

Anonymous

In the performance of a good action, a man not only benefits himself, but he confers a blessing upon others.

Sir Philip Sidney

There is only one proof of ability—
results. Men with ability in action
get results.

Harry F. Banks

Unity and victory are synonymous.

Samora Machel

Success comes to those who
become success conscious. Failure
comes to those who indifferently
allow themselves to become failure
conscious.

Napoleon Hill

If the life of a river depended only on the rainfall within the confines of its own banks, it would soon be dry. If the life of an individual depended solely on his own resources, he would soon fall. Be grateful for your tributaries.

Dr. William Arthur

It isn't the number of people
employed in a business that makes
it successful, it's the number
working.

Anonymous

The only way to help people is to
give them a chance to help
themselves.

Elbert Hubbard

Chance favors the prepared mind.

Louis Pasteur

The future belongs to the team
who lives intensely in the present.

Anonymous

It is the docile who achieve the
most impossible things in this
world.

Rabindranath Tagore

Teams are successful only when
they have the will and
determination to be so.

Anonymous

Set your goals high, and don't stop till you get there.

Bo Jackson

For all who make it, there's got to be a selflessness, a sublimination, automatically, of the individual to the whole.

Vince Lombardi

Working together brings out the best in us.

Anonymous

Inspiration and imagination go
hand in hand.

Anonymous

Every vital organization owes its
birth and life to an exciting and
daring idea.

James B. Conant

Purpose is the engine that fires
your dream and your team.

Anonymous

All who would win joy, must share it; happiness was born a twin.

Lord Byron

Life is like the car pool lane. The only way to get to your destination quickly is to take some people with you.

Peter Ward

He who has not faith in others shall find no faith in them.

Lao-tse

Combine two or more people in the pursuit of a common purpose and you can achieve more with less. Together we are able to accomplish what none of us could achieve alone.

Dan Zadra

We can do more than belong, we can participate.

Anonymous

You can dream, create, design, and build the most wonderful idea in the world, but it requires people to make the dream a reality.

Walt Disney

Very few burdens are heavy if everyone lifts.

Sy Wise

You will rise by lifting others.

Robert Green Ingersoll

In the game of hockey, it takes six to tango. You gotta stand up for your teammates.

Phil Esposito

This is the team. We're trying to go to the moon. If you can't put someone up, please don't put them down.

NASA motto

Tough times don't last—tough
people do.

Anonymous

Those with whom we work look to
us for heat as well as light.

Woodrow Wilson

Imagination can be creative or
destructive, depending upon
whether your team controls it or
lets it run wild.

Anonymous

Loyalty means not that I agree with everything you say, or that I believe you are always right. Loyalty means that I share a common ideal with you and that, regardless of minor differences, we strive for it, shoulder to shoulder, confident in one another's good faith, trust, constancy, and affection.

Dr. Karl Menninger

There is somebody smarter than
any of us, and that is all of us.

Michael Nolan

To get the full value of joy you
must have people to divide it with.

Mark Twain

The best hope of solving all our
problems lies in harnessing the
diversity, the energy, and the
creativity of all our people.

Roger Wilkins

A dedicated team is the fuel for
progress and growth.

Anonymous

If you don't invest very much, then
defeat doesn't hurt very much and
winning is not very exciting.

Dick Vermeil

Those who dare to fail miserably,
can achieve greatly.

Robert F. Kennedy

Combined thought has extra problem-solving powers.

Anonymous

The real winners are the people who look at every situation with an expectation that they can make it work or make it better.

Barbara Pletcher

We are what we believe we are.

Benjamin Cardozo

If we take people as they are, we make them worse. If we treat them as if they were what they ought to be, we help them to become what they are capable of becoming.

Goethe

It takes two wings for a bird to fly.

Jesse Jackson

There is a transcendent power
in example. We reform others
unconsciously when we walk
uprightly.

Anne Sophie Swetchine

Good work and good companions
are the building blocks of self-esteem.

Anonymous

Personal relationships are the fertile soil from which all advancement in real life grows.

Ben Stein

It is through cooperation, rather than conflict, that your greatest successes will be derived.

Ralph Charrell

Team energy multiplies when you set a desired goal and resolve to achieve it.

Anonymous

Many hands, hearts, and minds
generally contribute to anyone's
notable achievements.

Walt Disney

The future belongs to those that
believe in the beauty of their
dreams.

Eleanor Roosevelt

Great discoveries and achievements
invariably involve the cooperation
of many minds.

Alexander Graham Bell

P*eople must believe in each other, and feel that it can be done and must be done; in that way they are enormously strong. We must keep up each other's courage.*

Vincent Van Gogh

Joint undertakings stand a better chance.

Euripides

People acting together as a group can accomplish things which no individual acting alone could ever hope to bring about.

Franklin D. Roosevelt

The greatest good we can do for others is not to share our riches but to reveal theirs.

Anonymous

By uniting we stand, by
dividing we fall.

Joan Dickinson

The most important single
ingredient in the formula of
success is knowing how to get
along with people.

Thomas Roosevelt

A job worth doing is worth
doing together.

Anonymous

These other Successories® titles are available from Career Press:

➤ *The Magic of Motivation*

➤ *The Essence of Attitude*

➤ *The Power of Goals*

➤ *Commitment to Excellence*

➤ *The Best of Success*

To order call: 1-800-CAREER-1

These other Successories® titles are available from Career Press:

➤ *Great Little Book on The Gift of Self-Confidence*

➤ *Great Little Book on The Peak Performance Woman*

➤ *Great Little Book on Mastering Your Time*

➤ *Great Little Book on Effective Leadership*

➤ *Great Little Book on Personal Achievement*

➤ *Great Little Book on Successful Selling*

➤ *Great Little Book on Universal Laws of Success*

➤ *Great Quotes from Great Women*

➤ *Great Quotes from Great Sports Heroes*

➤ *Great Quotes from Great Leaders*

➤ *Great Quotes from Zig Ziglar*

To order call: 1-800-CAREER-1